Hugh Schpenus IV

Back for Vengeance

Back for War

Prologue

My Little Schpenus

"Oh, my little Schpenus," the woman said, caressing his head. "Look

at how big my little Schpenus has grown!"

The young boy smiled at his mother, "I wish papa was here. Where is

papa, mama?"

Her heart broke upon hearing her son's question. "I don't know where

your papa is, but when I find him, I will kill him myself!"

"Why, mama? Why would you do that?"

She looked down at her son with compassion, "Go now, go and play."

The young boy ran out of the house into the playground across the

street. Their home was a small shack that sat on the city's outskirts.

The woman stared out through the window observing her son

as she washed the dishes. Her heart ached at the emptiness within.

She wondered where he was. Her husband abandoned them. She

Hugh Schpenus IV

scowled. A growing storm brewed deep within her. A flaming fury of rage and spiraled like a tornado of hate. "I will find you one day, I will find you one day," she repeated softly.

The boy noticed his mother staring at him and waved gleefully, breaking the storm temporarily. She smiled and slowly returned the wave. Her heart still ached.

Chapter 1

Broken Moon

Stacy stood outside his home. It has been fifteen years since it all ended. Fifteen years since anyone heard or last saw Hugh Schpenus. It was rumored that he survived the plane crash. Michael Cleveland who simply went by Cleveland was the last person to see him alive. Now a police chief, Cleveland runs the department like Stacy used to. He smiled quietly under the light from the full moon

Hugh Schpenus IV

above. The November air was crisp. A mixture of vapor and cigarette smoke escaped his lungs as he exhaled. He lifted the half-smoked cigarette with two fingers and chuckled.

In front of him laid a blanket of forest and shrubbery. From years of being on the police force, his hardened instincts informed him that something or someone was out there watching him. Even in his early sixties, Stacy feared no one, not even death himself. Behind him, the curtains were drawn. Silhouettes of his family danced in front of the lights from inside his mahogany-colored house. He stood outside reminiscing of simpler times and days. Stacy missed sitting at his desk talking to Hugh Schpenus. Hugh Schpenus, what a name. What a guy. The most exemplary police officer and detective the world had ever known.

The last time he spoke to Hugh was when he was sent to Russia to rescue Cleveland. Hugh learned a terrible secret, the woman who kidnapped Cleveland was none other than his own mother. Simply known as Mama in the criminal underworld, she oversaw an entire operation running out of Russia. She had several connections, including Phucc Yue, who had been running his own operation in Bangkok, Thailand.

After Hugh traveled to Bangkok and stopped Phucc Yue, Mama sought out her own plate of vengeance. Unfortunately, stopping her cost Hugh Schpenus his own life. On his way back to West End with her, the airplane went down and the only survivor was Cleveland.

Suddenly the trees and shrubbery in front of Stacy began shaking wildly as if two animals were making love. But there was no love in front of him, only an unwanted and uninvited guest.

Stacy tried unholstering his firearm, only he realized his gun was inside tucked under the bed in a lockbox. He shook his head out of frustration.

"Damn retirement!" he exclaimed as a shadow approached him in front of the trees.

With a silencer gun in hand, the mysterious person stood in front of him dressed in all black with a black ski mask covering their face.

"I take it you're here to kill me?" Stacy assumingly asked while remaining calm. A part of him knew this day would arrive, especially after the first time someone tried to take his life. It was Oleg, one of Mama's henchmen. He shot him several times, but somehow Stacy survived. He survived the assassination attempt, but only to face another moment in front of another assassin who threatened to end his life.

"I am," answered the man. Apathy lingered in his voice.

Stacy smiled, "At least show me your face. Be a man."

Hugh Schpenus IV

The assassin tilted his head as if he was contemplating the unexpected request.

"Very well," he answered coldly. He removed his mask, revealing his face.

"Oh my god, is it really you? It can't be!" Stacy expressed while the half-smoked cigarette fell out of his mouth like a tumbling log.

Without further words, the man pointed the silencer at Stacy's head and fired a single shot. The snapping sound of the gun whispered as the bullet hit its target.

Stacy was dead.

Chapter 2

Ghosts from the Past

"I can't believe it. He is really dead!" Cleveland knelt over Stacy's body, shaking his head. "Who would do this?"

"We are still working out the details, sir," replied the female police officer.

"I want you to get me everything!" he demanded. "Whoever killed him will pay! Moments like this make me wish Schpenus was around," he sighed.

Hugh Schpenus IV

"Yes, sir!" answered the police officer as she began collecting evidence.

"And where is Jass? Have you seen Hugh Jass?"

"He was running late this morning," answered the same police officer.

Cleveland stood up and paced around like a rabid cougar. "Dammit! I am not having a good Friday. You know today is Friday, you know that, right, Kate?"

"Yes, sir, I do know today is Friday," she answered, noticing something peculiar. "Sir, I think I have something."

"What is it, Kate, and this better be damn good! I am not in the mood for trivial bs now."

"No sir, please, look at this!"

Cleveland knelt beside the blonde-haired woman and noticed what she was referring to. "Damn fine excellent work! You are damn impressive! My boy, Schpenus, would be proud of you!"

Kate blushed, "Thank you, sir, that means a lot to me. I look up to Schpenus. In fact, you can say he is my hero and why I joined the force."

Cleveland beamed delightfully, "Get this down to forensics, find out if there are any prints on that bullet casing."

"Yes, sir!" Kate answered while she saluted her boss.

Hugh Schpenus IV

Back at the office, Cleveland sat at his desk. His gray suitcoat rested on the back of his black leather chair. At the same time, the television that sat beside him on his desk showed a news anchor talking about Stacy's death. He looked at the news report and shook his head in disgust and grief. Tears began pooling in his eyes, forcing him to inhale deeply. The last thing Cleveland wanted to do was cry in front of his squad.

"We will all miss you, Stacy, your many years of service will not be forgotten," declared the news anchor.

The anchor's words conjured a harsh scoff from Cleveland. He shook his head, knowing it was just fluff. People will never know Stacy like he did because they served together as partners while cleaning up the streets of Detroit. In the eighties, crime was much different than it is now. The picture of him, Schpenus, and Stacy caught his attention. He lifted the brown picture frame from the corner of his desk and smiled. Schpenus, who resembled an eighties action star with his trademark white tank top and black leather jacket, stood in the middle of them both like a giant. Cleveland chuckled, remembering the first time they met in Bangkok at the Twisted Kitty. Schpenus was dressed like a Florida retiree in what he called "cruise wear," which was lost when he set foot in that city.

We had some good times, old buddy.

Hugh Schpenus IV

Cleveland placed the picture frame back down on his desk and looked at the only other photo he had of Schpenus. This was the photo he'd received in a letter shortly after the plane crash. The plane broke apart and plummeted hard into the ocean, causing a large explosion. The envelope contained no return address and was postmarked from Russia. Inside was a photo of Hugh as a young boy with his father, Andrei. On the back of the picture were the initials A.S. and H.M.S. Andrei Schpenus, and Hugh Mungis Schpenus.

A sudden knock on his door broke the nostalgic moment Cleveland was lost in.

"Sir, I am sorry to interrupt you, but detective Hugh Jass is here."

"Send him in here!" yelled Cleveland.

The man entered the room and plopped down in the metal chair in front of Cleveland's desk. He wore a black hoodie and blue jeans with black sneakers. His hair was a mixture of blonde and brown.

"Jass, Hugh Jass, you are late, again!" yelled Cleveland.

"I know, sir, I am sorry, sir."

"You are lucky I like you. You served in the military like me. You were a Major correct?"

"No sir, my first name is Hugh, but I was a sergeant, sir."

"Sergeant Jass," Cleveland declared and shook his head in disappointment. "Why were you late this morning, son?"

Hugh Schpenus IV

"Sir, I was late because my alarm was not set. I forgot daylight savings time ended, sir."

"Daylight savings time, what a joke that is. Someone once said, 'Only the government would believe that you can cut a foot off the top of a blanket, sew it to the bottom and get a longer blanket.' Have you heard this quote before, Hugh?"

The young man shook his head, "I have not, sir."

Cleveland stood up and casually walked over to the window and placed a toothpick inside his mouth. His salt and pepper facial hair was revealed clearer by the late morning sun. His bald head glistened under the artificial office lights.

"I am getting too old for this shit, son. I am not sure how much longer I can continue to babysit you."

"I understand, sir! It will not happen again, sir!"

Cleveland glanced over at Hugh and scoffed while adjusting his black-rimmed glasses, "Look at me," he began. "I am even wearing bifocals now. Can you believe that? I am barely in my fifties! How old are you?"

"I am thirty-five, sir. My birthday was last week."

"Thirty-five years old. When I was your age, I was living in Thailand. Now, I am here babysitting you. Something just isn't right."

Hugh Schpenus IV

"Sir, permission to speak freely?" the young man implored respectfully.

Cleveland returned to his desk and groaned softly as he sat down in his black leather chair. "Go ahead, kid. We're not in the military, so just be yourself."

"I believe what you are experiencing is something called a midlife crisis."

Upon hearing Hugh's statement, Cleveland could not help but laugh hysterically. "Midlife crisis, huh?" he repeated. "And what makes you say that?"

"Sir, I mean boss, I mean Cleveland, I understand what you are going through. The same happened to my father. Long story short, he left my mother, bought a Ferrari, and moved to Bolivia."

"And where is your father now?" Cleveland asked while tapping the eraser part of his yellow pencil gently against his desk. He was entertained by this young man's demeanor. Hugh was born in West End, and his mother, Tina, was a close associate to Cleveland. She worked undercover with Schpenus to take down one of West End's most notorious criminals, Carlos Dirty Sanchez.

"I do not know where my father is. This is all that my mother said to me."

Hugh Schpenus IV

Cleveland frowned at Hugh's response and speculated on whether or not she was telling him the truth. "I should call your mother. It has been some time since I've seen her. Is she still here in West End?"

"Yes, but she is planning on moving to another city. I am not sure where boss."

"Hmm, and when is she moving?"

"Next week."

"Next week? Why didn't you tell me this sooner? I will call her today. Maybe she will have time for a quick goodbye drink with me."

"That sounds like a plan, sir," he replied and winked at his boss.

"It is not like that, dummy. Would you really want me as your father?"

"Still speaking freely, sir, but no. You remind me of a Samuel Jackson kind of tough guy, and it is quite intimidating."

Hugh's response unexpectedly caused another laugh from Cleveland. "You know, I am not going to fire you today. After what I went through, our conversation cheered me up. I take that more as a compliment. I like Samuel, he is a good actor. Now go out there and detect. I need you to come up with some leads on who killed Stacy and why."

Hugh stood up at attention and saluted Cleveland, "I will find out as much as I can, sir!"

Hugh Schpenus IV

Chapter 3

The Grim Reaper

Hugh Schpenus IV

He sat in the dark living room of the tiny one-bedroom apartment on the brown leather couch. He continued cleaning his handgun over the dirty coffee table. Several gun parts and other weapons were scattered on the table. The news report continued to discuss the murder of Stacy on the television in front of him. "Funeral arrangements have been finalized, and we expect live coverage," the news anchor's words caught the man's attention. He looked up at the television screen and smiled. He rubbed his weathered face and nodded contently after seeing the image of the former police chief and commissioner on the screen with the word "killed" in red letters.

"He got what he deserved," he whispered gently, setting the gun on the table. His eyes glanced over at the large sniper rifle and automatic firearms. He rubbed his stubby chin with his fingers as if contemplating a decision.

Beside him, several black and white profile photos sat, including a photo of Stacy, with a large X marked in red marker coloring. A cigarette burned peacefully on the table in a glass ashtray. The man was slender but muscular for his size. His blonde hair was short and messy, eyes blue, focused on the photo of the next target. Tina Jass. His eyebrow perked at the attractiveness of her picture.

Hugh Schpenus IV

"Cuban mami. I hate to kill such a pretty lady, but I must do what I must do," he mocked sardonically. "I will be your grim reaper. I will bring death to all of your friends until I have my revenge."

The assassin tossed the photo down onto the others and focused on his weaponry. He wore black tactical gear, fingerless gloves, and black combat boots. His black ski mask was draped over the cracked leather armrest. Outside, lightning silently flickered as if heaven was taking a photo. This caught the man's attention causing him to stand up and walk over toward the window. The city of West End sat in the distance. Another flash flickered brightly, causing him to reminisce on another life. A life that felt so distant.

"I miss papa, mama," he said to the woman.

His questions provoked his mother, causing her to slap him as if he was misbehaving. Confused, the boy did not understand why his question warranted such a punishing reaction.

"Stop asking about your father! He is never coming home!" the mother angrily replied. "If you ask again, I will hit you!"

Afraid of receiving another thrashing, the young boy remained silent as the tears slowly rolled down his pale face. The side of his face, still red from where his mother slapped him, stung as the tears rolled down.

"I'm sorry I asked you this question mama, I will not ask again. I will not ask again!" he wailed loudly. "Papa is never coming home!"

The sentence echoed in his thoughts as he regained his attention to the present. He rubbed his eyes with his fingers and stepped away from the window. Rain lightly tapped against the glass as he walked over to the couch and began sharpening his black throwing daggers. "Rain is expected tonight in West End, so be sure to carry your umbrellas, folks!" the meteorologist declared while pointing at the map of the city where an animated rain cloud showed rain falling over large regions of the city.

The man laughed and scoffed at the television while he sharpened his blade. "No, really, you could have fooled me, weather guy. It is already raining."

Gently he placed the knives on the table and looked at Tina's photo again. Her eyes stared directly into his. "Should I kidnap you or kill you instead? The kidnapping may draw more attention than necessary and prolong the inevitable. I will decide after the funeral. The fools do not realize I am there, right there under their fat noses."

Chapter 4

Ghosts

Hugh Schpenus IV

The rain from the day before continued ravaging throughout the city. A strong torrent fell over the mourning crowd huddled together below. They sat under their black umbrellas on white plastic chairs. The rain was not the only thing falling on this day. It was also countless tears from the mourners who came to pay their respects to Stacy Jackson. The priest dressed in black with a matching black tippet that looked like a scarf than part of his ceremonial garments. "Today, we are all gathered here to mourn the passing of Stacy Jackson. It pains me to deliver this sermon because I was a close friend of this strong-willed man."

As the priest continued with his religious sermon, Cleveland, Jass, and his mother, Tina, sat several rows away. The rain loudly tapped and rattled against both the umbrellas and vacant plastic chairs, including the one beside Cleveland, which was reserved for Hugh Schpenus. Despite his friend's absence, he still somehow expected him to show up today. This was mainly because Stacy was also Hugh's closest friend, long-time mentor, and boss. And despite everyone's beliefs that Hugh was actually dead, Cleveland still refused to believe this.

"Do you think he will show?" Tina whispered to him.

Hugh Schpenus IV

"I don't know, but knowing my boy Schpenus, he probably won't come. He knows if he were to show up today, his sudden appearance would draw unwanted attention away from why we are really here."

"That is a good point," she replied. "I do not think your father is alive."

"I do, mom, just like dad," added Hugh.

She smiled thoughtfully at her son and said, "I don't know if your father is still out there, mijo. But regardless, he loves you very much."

"Tina, if you don't mind me asking, who is…" but before Cleveland could finish his question, the priest called him up.

"I believe a Michael Cleveland is present today and has something he would like to share about his friend Stacy Jackson."

"Ah, that's my cue, be right back!" he said.

A heavy sigh escaped him as he stood in front of the small crowd. Behind them, news cameras focused their attention on him.

"Today, we are here to remember the passing of a great man, Stacy Jackson. It feels like just yesterday when I first met him. Together we took down many, many criminals in the streets of Detroit. Everything this man taught me," he said while gently pounding his chest. "I still carry today and believe in his words of justice, honesty, and respect. We have to respect our fellow humans, but we have to respect the law most of all. It feels like just yesterday that we were gathered here to mourn the passing of another individual," he paused and briefly looked

Hugh Schpenus IV

up. His eyes scanned the crowd in hopes of seeing a glimpse of Schpenus.

In the distance through the heavy torrent, his eyes caught the sight of a man leaning against a tree. The resemblance to Schpenus was almost uncanny, and it was like he saw a ghost. The mourners began looking at each other and whispering as Cleveland broke stride and lost his train of thought. He rubbed his eyes and looked again toward the tree, but the figure was gone.

"Sorry, I am just seeing ghosts," he abruptly stated. "It feels like just yesterday we were gathered here to mourn the passing of Hugh Schpenus. But now, with the passing of Stacy Jackson, it seems our city has lost not only two great men but heroes as well. But fear not, West Enders, I promise you today that I will find out who is behind this gruesome murder! This crime will not go unpunished!"

The sudden statement and announcement brought a mixture of praise and shock from the mourning crowd. As Cleveland stepped away from the makeshift podium, several people stood up, clapped, and cheered. The rain did not distract or bother them as he walked down the aisle smiling and respectfully waving and nodding at fellow mourners.

"Wow, what a great speech!" Hugh declared as Cleveland joined him and Tina.

Hugh Schpenus IV

"Thanks, kid, I appreciate that."

"Did you really mean what you said?" Tina cautiously asked.

"About catching the criminal. Yes, we will find out who is behind this."

"But we don't have any leads yet, boss," added Hugh.

"I know, but have faith," declared Cleveland. He rubbed his eyes again and turned around, glancing over at the tree.

"What is it?" Tina asked.

"You know, ah, nothing. It's nothing. I thought I saw someone familiar, that's all."

She smiled at him, "I know. I miss him, too."

"Say, Tina, what are you doing Friday? Your son here told me you were moving out of West End. You weren't planning on leaving without saying goodbye now, were you?"

She blushed at Cleveland, "I wasn't going to tell anyone really. I am sorry, it's been tough on me ever since he…" her voice lingered.

"I know. I miss him, too," he stated as they both smiled in concert.

"Let's meet for drinks?"

Tina nodded, "That sounds nice."

"Great, Friday, seven at Broken Pistol. It's that new place down by the harbor."

Hugh Schpenus IV

"I have not been there yet but heard it was a happening spot. Look at you, Cleveland, still living your youthful days just like in…where was it? Korea?"

He chuckled, "Thailand, and yeah, I suppose you could say that."

"Oh Cleveland, some things never change. Don't ever change, okay?"

He laughed softly at Tina, "You got it. I won't."

Chapter 5

Cemetery Ghost

The scent of freshly cut grass lingered in the air. Cleveland stepped carefully as he trekked through Heaven's Gate Cemetery. His gray dress pants brushed lightly against the green shards. He carried a large stand with flowers that read "miss you." Behind him, detective Jass followed him. Ever since the young officer joined the squad ten years ago, Cleveland made it a point to take him under his wing. He decided not by choice but because of a promise he made to his mother, Tina. A part of her was against him joining the police force, but she knew it wouldn't be right to stop her son from fulfilling his

Hugh Schpenus IV

dreams. To add further protection and guidance, she made Cleveland promise her that he would always watch over her son.

"Sir?" Hugh cautiously asked.

"What is it, son?" he replied, stopping abruptly in front of the headstone.

"Are you going on a date with my mother tonight?"

The sudden and inappropriate question caused a frustrated exhale as he placed the flowers beside the headstone.

"This is for you, buddy. You will never be forgotten ever," he declared.

"You know, I met him, Stacy Jackson. He was a great guy. He told me something that I will never forget."

"Yeah? What's that?" he asked Hugh while still focused on Stacy's headstone. His eyes read focused on the quote, *never stop fighting because crime never stops,* above the date of birth and death range.

"He said to me, Hugh Jass, don't let me down, don't let the squad down, and most of all, don't let Cleveland down."

Surprised by Hugh's words, Cleveland turned around and smiled at him, "You are doing great,

son, don't you worry. I know that I am not always the nicest guy around, but —"

"I understand," he interrupted. "To be honest with you, Cleveland, I see you…." he paused to

build up the courage and heart to say it. "I see you as a father figure."

Hugh Schpenus IV

The young man's unexpected words left him speechless. "Thank you, Hugh, that means a lot to me. I won't let you down either."

Cleveland decided it was time for his young detective to focus on the mission with the heavy sentimental air between them.

"Listen, it has been a week since Stacy's murder. We have to focus our efforts on catching his killer. Head back to the crime scene and search for any clues. Let's meet back in the office in the evening."

"Before your date with my mom?" he responded with a smile.

Cleveland chuckled and shook his dead. "I will meet you back at the office. I still need to do one more thing here."

"You got it, boss."

As he watched Jass return to his car, Cleveland exhaled a heavy sigh. A heavy dose of sadness slapped him like an angry woman. It was time to visit another grave, the grave of an old friend. Unlike Stacy's grave, standing in front of the grave for Hugh Schpenus felt different. It felt empty. He missed Stacy and Hugh Schpenus. Something inside told him Schpenus was still alive. Gently, Cleveland placed a small decorative "miss you" sign beside the grave. Seeing the headstone with his name made the hard-nose detective doubt that his friend was really dead. The gentle rustle from the leaves of the nearby whispering willow tree broke his attention.

Hugh Schpenus IV

Realizing it was time to return to the office, Cleveland turned and headed back to his car, carrying a heavy dosage of doubt and denial. About halfway to his vehicle, a strange feeling that someone was watching him abruptly paused the man in his tracks. He looked up and decided to give Hugh's grave one last look.

In front of Hugh Schpenus' grave site stood a figure of a man who resembled his fallen friend. Cleveland could not believe his eyes. The strange sight of the man left him feeling petrified. He stood there wearing a black leather jacket, a white tank top, and blue jeans. His short blonde hair was messy and disheveled. He felt a strange, unsettling sensation seeing the man who resembled Hugh Schpenus who stood there like a statue, staring at him. Cleveland closed his eyes and shook his head in hopes of shaking off this weird haunting sight. After he opened his eyes, the man was gone.

"I must be losing my damn mind!" he declared quietly. "No, no, that wasn't him. I need…"

Cleveland was about to head back to the vehicle when something struck the hard-nosed detective. If someone was really at his grave, he would find footprints. As he took the first step toward the grave, a cold breeze passed, almost like it was pushing him back and warning him.

Hugh Schpenus IV

"No, I am not going to check. I need to get back to the office,"

Cleveland quietly declared. "I will be back, Schpenus."

Chapter 6

Clues

The yellow caution tape flapped and rattled wildly in the wind.

Dressed in his signature black hoodie and black jeans, Detective Jass

returned to the scene of the crime. Thanks to it being early in the

afternoon, the sun shined over him, providing him with an ample amount of light. Even though it was a week since Stacy was murdered, remnants from his murder still lingered. He found dried blood still caked on both the grass and mud. The blood almost blended into the soil, and it could easily be missed by the naked eye, but not for Hugh.

He liked to think he was a good detective.

Despite it being a week later, Cleveland hoped sending his young detective here would help unravel and uncover clues for finding out who was behind Stacy's murder. Jass did not want to let his boss down. He rubbed his smooth tan chin. Part of the hoodie he wore covered his blondish brown hair, which was short and messy. "Okay, time to find some evidence," he said softly.

It was pretty taxing for both the detectives and forensic team to find any solid leads and evidence because of where the crime occurred. The area was small and concentrated, making it more accessible. But the passing storms and muddy terrain made it difficult to find anything. Most of the team assumed it was all ruined from the autumn storms.

Cleveland disagreed and knew there had to be something. This same infectious belief was passed down to the young detective, who also carried the same sentiment. His eyes danced around the scene. Inside his thoughts, Hugh began reimaging and replaying the

Hugh Schpenus IV

crime. He stood exactly where Stacy stood the night he was murdered. Noticing the forestry in front of him, the young man realized the killer must have traveled from the depths of the forest.

"Well, I might as well take a look inside the forest," he said aloud.

Leaves and twigs crunched beneath his sneakers, which he realized was not the best choice of attire for trekking through the woods. As he walked into the forest, he imagined the killer doing the same after murdering Stacy. With every step he took, Hugh looked around in hopes of finding the killer's footprints. Unfortunately, it was proving difficult to find any prints a week later.

The young detective found a large clearing ahead after making his way deeper into the forest. The terrain consisted of earth, fallen leaves, and twigs, but something else caught his eye, tire marks. Not just any tire marks because these belonged to a motorcycle. Hugh knelt down and took several photos of the motorcycle tire marks with his digital camera. What was peculiar about the tire marks was they belonged to a racing motorcycle. It was most perplexing how the assassin managed to bring this bike so far into the forest.

The sound of a passing car suddenly caught his attention. He stood up and continued through the clearing. With every step he took, the sound of the passing cars became louder and louder. Something was not adding up to Hugh, but he was determined to solve the mystery. As he walked alongside the motorcycle track, the young detective discovered another clue about the assassin. They did not ride their motorcycle into the forest but instead walked and left it at the clearing. This explains why they traveled on foot and how they managed to catch Stacy by surprise. This assassin must have been tracking and watching him for quite some time, which means this was a planned assassination.

After following the track for another mile, Hugh found himself standing in front of a road. The motorcycle track ended at the opening into the forest. Several cars zoomed by in front of him as he stood there observing the area. He felt proud of finding this critical clue since this narrowed down who the killer could be. This killer planned the assassination because it seemed like the person who committed the crime was out for revenge.

Satisfied with the results from his search for new clues, Hugh trekked back into the forest and returned to the scene of the crime. With the sunlight shining on another spot near the crime scene, something that went unnoticed caught his eye. Standing several feet away from where Stacy was shot, the detective found another critical piece of evidence. Hidden and barely noticeable were five thin strands of blonde hair tucked away beneath a half-turned stone. Jass felt astonished that he could spot this from his vantage point. He carefully picked them up and placed them in evidence bags, then safely tucked them away into his pocket.

Chapter 7

Hugh Schpenus IV

Evidence

Cleveland used to see moments like tonight differently during his younger days. Meeting an attractive woman for a drink usually meant a more romantic evening than tonight, which was strictly casual and business. His agenda for that night was to cherish the memories they both shared, especially the memories with Hugh Schpenus. Tina was a great detective, and a part of him wished she was still on the force. She spent five years working undercover to take down one of West End's most notorious and famous crime lords, Carlos Dirty Sanchez.

It was a surprise that she was working undercover. No one on the force knew her true identity, except for one person, Stacy Jackson. Cleveland wanted to talk to her about her experience working undercover. He buttoned up his matching gray suitcoat and flipped his newsboy cap onto his shiny head.

Damn I still got it! I look like a better version of Mr. Clean! I could have been Mr. Clean even when I had an afro. Just call me Mr. Afro! Hot damn, I could have marketed sponges now that I think about it, he said aloud to himself and laughed excitedly.

Hugh Schpenus IV

"You sure could have, sir," announced Kate, standing at the open doorway.

Embarrassed by the unexpected eavesdropper, Cleveland smiled and cleared his throat. "I apologize for that display of unprofessionalism, Katerini."

The young woman smiled affectionately at her boss and waved her hand, "It's okay, sir. I just wanted to tell you that Hugh returned with some key evidence."

"Oh did he now?" he perked an eyebrow while adjusting the crimson silk tie over his white shirt. "How does this look? Do you see my bulletproof vest?"

Kate gasped and covered her mouth, "You're wearing your bulletproof vest on a date, sir?"

He laughed at her question, "Can't be too sure these days, and I always like to have protection."

She chuckled at his answer. "Usually, the men I have gone on dates with carry another kind of protection, sir."

"Right! You reminded me. I better not forget that!" he declared.

She nodded shyly as her boss reached into his desk, but to her surprise, he pulled out something unexpected, a small handgun.

"Can't leave without this!" he exclaimed while tucking the small firearm into his back waist.

Hugh Schpenus IV

"That's not the type of protection…" the young woman sighed and shook her head. "Jass is waiting for you in his office."

"Understood, thank you, Kate. Oh, and by the way," he said, following her out of his office. "This is not a date."

"Sure, got it, sir," she answered doubtfully.

"Got something for me?" Cleveland asked, gently knocking on Hugh's door.

"Sir, you are not going to believe what I found!" the young detective answered proudly.

"Well, spill the beans, kid. What did you find?"

"Sir," he starts, standing up proudly. "Take a look at this," he adds, giving Cleveland the digital camera.

"These cameras," he embarrassingly admits. "I have no idea how to work these things. You can call me a dinosaur all you want, but nothing beats a polaroid. This is what we used when I was your age."

"Sir, what year was this again?" he politely asked.

"It was in the sometime in the eighties, okay?" he replied with slight annoyance.

The unexpected reaction caused uncontrollable laughter from the young detective. He took the digital camera away from his boss and began pressing buttons on it. After a short pause, he handed the camera back to Cleveland.

Hugh Schpenus IV

"Here, sir, take a look at this," he said then pointed at the camera's screen. "This is the first clue that I found."

"Is that…" he paused with furrowed eyebrows. "Tire tracks?"

"Yes, sir, but not just any tracks. These belong to a racing motorcycle. I am guessing a Ducati of some sort."

"A what-ati?" Cleveland asked, handing the camera back to his young detective.

He chuckled softly at the question, "It is a motorcycle that can reach high speeds. But that's not all I found sir, I also found this!" Hugh Jass grabbed a small evidence bag from his pocket and tossed it over to his boss.

"What is this?" he hesitated while inspecting the bag. "Hair?"

"Correct, sir, it is a blonde lock of hair. I am unsure who this belongs to, but I am going to take this down to forensics."

Cleveland looked up and tossed the bag back to his detective. "Wow, this is some damn fine detective work. I cannot believe this was at the crime scene. Get this down right away to the evidence room. I want the results as soon as possible."

"Yes, sir."

"Now, if you'll excuse me, I am going to go meet your mother for drinks."

"Have fun, sir," replied Hugh Jass. Do you need backup, sir?"

Hugh Schpenus IV

Cleveland smiled and shook his head, "That won't be necessary, son."

"Understood, sir, be careful."

Chapter 8

Soup

He stood in front of the bathroom mirror inside the small hotel room. Cigarette smoke rose up beside as his blue eyes stared at his own reflection. He smiled. Tonight was the night he was going to make another guest appearance. On the left side corner of the white, porcelain sink sat his tool for the job tonight, a nine-millimeter pistol with a silencer attached to its barrel. Black like the evil lurking within his heart, the assassin held no second doubts or hesitation about his target tonight, Tina Jass.

Hugh Schpenus IV

The man was well aware of what she was capable of, and why she was leaving town. Like him, she carried her own secretive demons and snakes. He chuckled lightly as his white tank top rested against his bulging muscles. Having just completed an intense workout, the man was feeling euphoric. Like a ghost he has been haunting and toying his main target, but tonight he was going hunting.

He lifted the gun from the sink, which clung softly and aimed it at his own reflection. The assassin began laughing loudly, lowering the gun to his side against his leg. A sudden knock on the door broke his attention.

"Room service," the voice called out.

"Be right there," he said. He then exited the bathroom and tucked his weapon into his jeans.

The door opened and a young man stood in front of a long white dinner cart containing several dishes including a plate of grilled chicken kabobs, a bowl of borscht, and a round plate with a baked potato.

"Where would you like it sir?" the hotel employee respectfully asked.

"Leave it here, I will bring it in myself."

"That accent, are you German?"

The man smiled, "Something like that, here." he handed the employee a folded hundred-dollar bill.

Hugh Schpenus IV

"Wow really? Thank you, sir! Enjoy your meal!"

The assassin rolled the cart into the room and began chowing down on the meal. Everything was cooked perfectly except for the bowl of soup. After tasting it, the man frowned in disappointment. "This is what they call borscht? This tastes like canned soup!" he declared, pushing the bowl aside.

The television blared loudly with the football game on the screen, but he was not interested in watching. Instead, he focused on the meal and stared at the photo of Tina. He knew the time and location of where she was going to be. Tonight was not only about timing the attack perfectly, but it was also about sending a message. After the meal, he flung his black leather jacket around his body and grabbed several ammo clips for his handgun. It was time to go to work.

In order to avoid being spotted on surveillance cameras, the assassin exited his room and then proceed down to the garage through the stairwell. His boots echoed loudly as he stomped heavily down the grated metal stairs. In the garage his black Ducati 740 sat waiting for him like an obedient leopard. Its engine roared loudly as the bike came to life. The exhaust sounded like an angry savage swarm of bees as the bike exited from the parking garage.
His face and identity remained hidden beneath his black ski mask.

Hugh Schpenus IV

Chapter 9

Drinks

Cleveland stepped inside the bar, the Broken Pistol, only to see the place was bustling with the usual Friday night crowd. People sat around drinking and laughing while the football game played silently on the surrounding television screens. People in West End were not big into their football sports team, The Sturdy Endies, because the name sounded too close to The Dirty Undies. The team carried the worst team record and their quarterback, Tony Cunningham was known as Turnover Tony around town.

Tina sat alone at a red booth tucked away in the corner of the restaurant area where patrons munched on bar snacks and food such as burgers, pizza, and crispy chicken tenders. The crowd consisted of mixed ages ranging from early twenty-somethings to middle agers. Cleveland could distinguish their ages by their beverage choices. Young millennials as they were called, held craft beers and mixed beverages while the older crowd carried signature beers such as the ever so popular West Ender. The beer was the best thing the city

Hugh Schpenus IV

invented next to insult, pencil stuffer, which was mainly geared toward the snobby stock traders.

"Excuse me miss, but is this seat taken?" he politely asked.

His question invoked a light chuckle from the woman who wore a beautiful silver tight dress. Her wavy light brown hair sat above her shoulders. The red nail polish caught Cleveland's eyes briefly as he admired her alluring physique. Her light brown skin looked smooth, but he resisted the temptation of drawing in too close to the woman. There was a rumor that her and Hugh were lovers, but this was only speculated since he had many lovers during his time in West End.

A round and clear glass candle holder sat between them on the rose-colored tablecloth. The flame flickered slowly as the wax slowly disappeared. Despite the crowded atmosphere, the restaurant area was quite tame. Glasses and plates clinked and clanged as Cleveland and Tina laughed and chatted with initial small talk.

"Hello, welcome to the Broken Pistol, my name is Neil Jindal and I will be your waiter this fine evening," said the young man, who was dressed in a black t-shirt with the restaurant's logo of a broken gun. "May I start you fine folks with an adult beverage? Or perhaps something to munch on? I recommend the chicken poppers." Cleveland tilted his head and scowled slightly, "Chicken poppers? What is that?"

Hugh Schpenus IV

Neil, who looked to be in his late twenties, smiled excitedly, "Oh, yes, they are so good! So, we take the best part of the chicken and mix them with our secret spices including jalapenos. The best part, we fry them up, and with one bite they just pop in your mouth!" Cleveland exchanged a brief glance with Tina, who smiled nervously at the hardnose police chief. "All right, what the hell, let's try these popper things."

"Excellent choice sir, I promise you, you will like it! I eat them all the time. And for an adult beverage? May I suggest the Dirty Undie? It's our newest drink and on special tonight!" his voice was more excited than necessary in hopes of enticing the two patrons. Cleveland shook his head and gently touched his forehead. "I will have a classic, give me a vintage style."

"Excellent choice sir, my grandfather loves that beer!" Neil's unintentional insult brought a chuckle from Tina. "And you miss?"

"Just give me a five-dollar margarita please."

"Excellent! Okay I will return with your drinks and chicken poppers shortly."

After the waiter disappeared into the kitchen, Cleveland looked over at Tina, who exploded in heavy laughter.

"Are you telling me I am that old that my favorite beer is now considered a grandfather drink? I am only fifty-five!"

Hugh Schpenus IV

Tina shook her head as she smiled and laughed softly, "Oh, Cleveland, it happens you know?"

"What does?"

"Getting old. Times are changing. Life is like a roller coaster and we're just here for the ride."

"You're telling me life is a roller coaster. Can you believe how much has changed? When we were busting crime it was much easier. Now with the computers and the internet."

Tina nodded in agreement, "I will admit, it has become a bit more complicated, but at the same time there is a convenience. We have cellular phones now. Do you know what that means?"

Cleveland scoffed, "Yeah, now I can take my calls from the toilet."

His response made Tina erupt in heavy laughter, "Oh, Cleveland, never change. You always find a way to cheer me up."

"Cheer you up? Oh, is it the move?"

Her laughter faded replaced by a somber smile. "For every moment filled with laughter, there are tears falling somewhere else."

"And hello there, folks," Neil interrupted, placing a red plastic basket with a blanket of clear parchment paper. On top a dozen round fried chicken balls sat within. The smell of grease and jalapeno permeated between them. "Here are your drinks," the waiter added placing a large beer stein containing the amber fluid and a fancy margarita

Hugh Schpenus IV

goblet with a clear liquid. "Enjoy your drinks and munchies!" he excitedly proclaimed.

"Well," added Cleveland. "Time to dive in."

Chapter 10

The Masked Rider

"So, what did you think about the poppers?" Neil excitedly asked.

"They were…" Cleveland hesitated to answer.

Hugh Schpenus IV

"Good," said Tina and Cleveland in concert.

"Awesome! See, I knew you would like them! Is there anything else you would like?"

"No, just the check please," he politely asked the young waiter.

"Sounds good, I'll be right back with the bill," Neil answered while pointing happily at Cleveland.

After the waiter disappeared into the sea of patrons, Cleveland chugged the last of his second beer in hopes of washing down the awful remnants of jalapeno and grease. Tina followed suit and finished her margarita. He slammed the glass down on the table causing a light thump and exhaled heavily.

"I don't know about you, but damn that was spicy. I don't think I'll be popping back here anytime soon."

Cleveland's words caused a chuckle from Tina. "Oh, Cleveland, I am going to miss you," she finally admitted.

"Tina, if you don't mind me asking, why are you skipping town? What about your son?"

She sighed in response to Cleveland's question.

"My son grew up so fast. He can handle his own, and plus, Hugh has you here looking after him. You're like the father he should have had."

"That reminds me, I wanted to ask you," he began to say.

Hugh Schpenus IV

"And here is your bill, I will leave this right here. Pay me whenever you want, no rush folks," Neil politely stated.

Annoyed by the waiter's sudden interruption, Cleveland shoved his silver credit card into the plastic sleeve and handed it to the young man.

"Okay then, I will be right back!" the waiter declared as he walked away from the table.

"Thank you for a lovely evening, I really enjoyed this," said Tina. A hint of sadness lingered in her voice.

Feeling annoyed that he lost his moment to ask her the question he originally wanted to ask, Cleveland decided another approach.

"Listen, Tina, are you sure you won't reconsider? West End just won't be the same without you."

She blushed, "Thanks, but hey, let's keep in touch. My cellphone number won't change anyway," she added with a light giggle.

He shook his head and laughed, "Cellphone, I can't get over these things."

"And here you go sir, thank you so much, I am really happy you enjoyed your time here," Neil respectfully gave Cleveland the bill containing the receipt and his credit card.

Together, they navigated through the crowded restaurant and bar area. The chilly late November air greeted them as they stepped

Hugh Schpenus IV

outside. The parking lot was still bustling, but mostly with people leaving the restaurant.

"Do you want a ride home?" Cleveland politely asked.

Tina smiled and shook her head, "No, thank you. I will walk a little to get some air and catch a cab."

Feeling concerned for her plan, he offered again, "Are you sure? I don't mind, you're on the way anyway to this burrito spot I am thinking about hitting. You may have heard of it. It's called Time for Tacos."

Cleveland's remark brought a chuckle, "Still hungry huh? Yeah, I am a little, too, but a burrito sounds too heavy."

"The tacos are good, too, but I won't push it."

"Thank you, Cleveland, but I will take a rain check," she said and hugged him tightly. "This isn't goodbye either, but a see you later okay?"

He smiled, "See you around Tina, watch yourself okay?"

"I will."

As the two parted ways, the sound of a black racing motorcycle filled the Friday night air like an angry hawk. The rider carefully veered the vehicle into the parking lot causing a car to narrowly miss it. The driver furiously honked the horn forcing Cleveland's attention on the rider, who stood out like a broken lightbulb in a lamp store. Through his black ski mask, the rider's blue

Hugh Schpenus IV

eyes briefly made contact with Cleveland's eyes. Seeing the strange mask rider gave him a strange feeling of familiarity. It was almost like he knew who it was beneath the mask.

It all happened in almost slow motion. The masked rider slowly pulled out the silencer from his side and aimed it at Tina, who was still focused on her own thoughts and not noticing what the rider was doing. Cleveland stood in disbelief at the scene unfolding before him. A part of him could not believe this was really happening.

"Tina! Look out!" Cleveland cried out as he galloped toward his friend.

The woman's eyes locked with the mask rider's as he slowed down and squeezed the trigger. Sparks of gunfire shot out from the long black suppressor. As the casings flipped up and out from the top of the gun, the bullets whizzed out hitting Tina's body. Slowly she collapsed onto the pavement. Cleveland caught her head and upper back as the masked rider drove away. He wanted to return gunfire, but instead, he chose to spend his last moments with Tina.

"Oh, Cleveland," she weakly said. "It looks like…I won't be eating those tacos with you after all."

Her words caused him to laugh while tears rolled down his face. "It's alright, they were terrible anyway."

"Listen, Cleveland. Watch over my son, okay?"

"Sure, anything, I will."

Hugh Schpenus IV

"He…means well, but he is just like his father…"

"Tina, who is his father?"

As her eyes slowly closed, she whispered, "Schpenus…father…"

Hugh Schpenus IV

Chapter 11

Early Riser

"Whoa! What the hell is going on?" Cleveland asked. He gripped the top of the brown leather seat.

"The plane is going down!" I yelled. "We need to get out of here."

"Whatever the reason, I am not ready to die! There are so many babes I need to see in Thailand. I can't die yet, Hugh Mungis Schpenus!" Cleveland frantically declared.

I shook my head at my friend, "You know if it was anyone else, and if we were not about to die, I would object to that name! You know part of that name belongs to my mother. My mother is Mungis. I am just a Hugh Schpenus."

Hugh Schpenus IV

Cleveland laughed, "Yeah whatever, man. Come on, let's find some parachutes and get out of here!"

Together we moved forward toward the cockpit gripping the top of the hard, brown leather chairs. A loud whirring sound echoed through the cabin as the plane continued its heavy descent.

"They must be in here!" Cleveland proclaimed as he opened a small closet. "Yes! I found…"

"Yes, you found?" I asked while making my way toward his side.

"One. There's only one parachute, man. What do we do? Flip for it?"

I shook my head and said, "No man, take it. Get out of here!"

Cleveland opened his eyes. His back was drenched in a heavy mixture of sweat and fear. It was just a dream, but unfortunately for him, it was a dream that really happened. That was the last time he saw Hugh Schpenus. He remembered that moment as if it happened yesterday. The plane broke apart as it crashed into the ocean, followed by an enormous thundering explosion. A part of him still believed he was still alive.

It has been over one month since Tina's murder, which was an assassination. Her killer was still out there on the loose, but so far,

Hugh Schpenus IV

they have gone into hiding. The haunting eyes still replayed like a broken reel in his head. They looked so familiar, but something was missing from them. He looked over at his watch and saw it was four in the morning. What an odd time to be awake. It was not exactly the best time to be awake since nothing was open outside. The only people who were out at this hour were early risers and criminals. The abrupt ringing of his telephone startled Cleveland. Who could be calling him at this hour?

"Hello?" he asked hoarsely on the phone. His voice still in its own slumber.

"Sir? Sorry to bother you at such an odd hour, but I received a call back from forensics. They were quite adamant about having you involved right away. You are not going to believe this." Hugh's voice was low and drenched in heavy sadness. He still mourned the unexpected passing of his mother, Tina.

Cleveland cleared his throat, "Tell me, what did they find out?"

"I would rather not discuss this over the phone. Do you mind meeting me at the office? I know it's an odd request, but…" his voice trailed off.

"It's fine son, I will meet you there in an hour. I have to get ready," his boss replied.

Hugh Schpenus IV

"Do you want me to pick you up one of those muffins with eggs? I heard they are quite tasty sir."

Cleveland exhaled softly and smiled, "That would be great. See you in an hour."

The streets were empty, and the roads were glazed like a ham on Christmas. An eerie air hung over the downtown area of West End. Street lights flashed from red to green as the street lights slowly dimmed. Cleveland never did like driving at this time of day. Despite it being almost five in the morning, the streets were still empty because it was a Sunday. His stomach grumbled like a bear waking from six months of slumber. That breakfast muffin sounded quite enticing despite its terrible taste.

As he approached closer to the police station, the sound of a motorcycle echoed from a nearby vacant parking garage belonged to Layers, a well-known department store. At first, Cleveland ignored it thinking it was just someone who arrived early at work until he caught a glimpse of the motorcycle and its rider. The black motorcycle stopped precisely in view when he stopped at the red traffic light. Like a red-light district special, Cleveland looked away from the light and locked eyes with the masked rider. Despite the distance of several

Hugh Schpenus IV

meters between them, he recognized it was the same assassin who killed Tina, and he most likely killed Stacy, too.

The rider slowly nodded as if he acknowledged or challenged the police chief. Cleveland knew this was not happening by accident or coincidence. This killer knew exactly when and where he was going to be. Like a sinful temptation, the rider sat on the second level of the parking garage and began revving his motorcycle. The engine of the Ducati came to life like a ravenous beast. It sounded like a million bees were swarming in the parking garage.

Chapter 12

Chasing a Ghost

Unable to resist the temptation, Cleveland succumbed and knew this was an opportune time to pursue the assassin. He quickly

Hugh Schpenus IV

jerked the steering wheel and drove toward the parking garage. The rider sat on his motorcycle and continued revving his Ducati, like a matador in front of an enraged bull. Letting his hate and rage take control and hold like a bloodthirsty savage, his black 97 Pontiac Grand Prix entered the lower level of the parking garage.

The sound of squealing wheels reverberated against the concrete walls as he navigated the oversized vehicle up the ramp toward the first level. The sound of the Ducati's engine and exhaust grew louder as Cleveland drove closer to his target. As his car raced through the first level, the sound of the motorcycle slowly faded, but he did not notice this since his determination was focused on reaching the second level of the parking garage.

Upon reaching his destination, Cleveland's mouth dropped wide open because to his surprise, the motorcycle was gone. The brakes chirped and the tires squealed as the vehicle came to a screeching halt near where the masked rider was. Before exiting from his car, he opened the glove box and grabbed a small loaded revolver. He exhaled deeply in hopes of calming his nerves. The last time Cleveland felt this nervous was when it was his first day on the job in Detroit. Back then he was a soft sponge learning everything there was to know about being a detective.

Hugh Schpenus IV

With his flashlight and revolver gun in hand, he combed through the area where the motorcycle was first seen. Unfortunately, the flashlight provided an insufficient amount of light because he was unable to see anything. The clinging of a can bouncing against the concrete in the distance caught his attention. Cleveland quickly shined his metal flashlight in the direction of where the noise originated from, but the light dimmed and weakened thanks to the dying batteries inside.

"Damn! Stupid flashlight! Why now?" his loud voice echoed within the vacant garage.

"You should have brought more batteries," the strange but familiar voice replied.

"Where are you? Show yourself!" Cleveland yelled out and waved his flashlight as if it were a magic wand.

"I'm right here!" the voice declared from behind him.

Cleveland spun around and aimed his light at the shadows in front of him. Two large concrete pillars with faded painted numbers hid whoever was hiding.

Hugh Schpenus IV

"Show yourself! Don't be a coward!" Cleveland yelled out, reluctancy kept him in his place.

The man laughed haughty, "It is not time yet, my friend."

"Who are you? Tell me who you are!" Cleveland ordered.

"You already know, who I am," the man simply replied as the engine of his motorcycle came to life.

"Schpenus? Is that you?" he asked, perplexity saturated his voice.

It was so dark in the garage that the motorcycle blended in perfectly with the shadows from the pillars. If it was not for the loud roar from the exhaust, Cleveland would not have known the mysterious man sped away. Frustrated at the sound of the masked rider speeding down the parking garage ramp, the tired police chief sighed and quickly returned to his car. He tossed the gun on the seat beside him and started his car.

The wheels chirped as he sped down the parking garage in hopes of catching up to the rider. It felt longer to reach the bottom of the garage, beads of sweat rolled down the sides of his face. That voice felt so familiar yet eerily different to him. The sound of the motorcycle faded with every turn it was lost completely as Cleveland

Hugh Schpenus IV

exited from the parking garage. A part of him was not surprised that this is how it ended.

Chapter 13

Turning Point

Hugh Schpenus IV

As the sun painted the morning sky with its light-yellow hues, frustration continued to build within Cleveland. He was becoming a ticking timebomb of anger and despair. He hoped whatever the evidence Hugh Jass wanted to tell him about was worth not only waking up this early in the morning, but worth chasing a ghost. Another sigh escaped the aging man. Deep down inside he knew he was getting too old for this sort of thing, even if he did not want to verbally admit it.

Cleveland entered the darkened police station. The door squeaked lightly as it closed behind him. There were no other signs of anyone else in the station. He flicked on the lights and saw Jass waiting for him in his office. His face was a mixture of sadness and sleepless nights. Cleveland shook his head at the poor sight of the kid.

"Hey, son, I am here," he calmly stated.

"Sir," he replied. In his hands Hugh Jass clutched a manila envelope. "Here sir, this is for you." he handed Cleveland the envelope. "I also have your breakfast here," he said, then placed the brown bag on the desk.

Hugh Schpenus IV

Cleveland ignored the bag containing the muffin and instead focused on the envelope as he sat at his desk.

"Are you okay sir?" Hugh asked noticing the man's face and attire was damp.

"Yeah, you can say I had a rough morning," he answered, not wanting to go into details about his ordeal at the parking garage. "Let's see what's inside," he said calmly and opened the envelope. His thoughts were elsewhere, still fixated on the masked rider he unexpectedly encountered in the parking lot.

Cleveland's face scowled as he began reading the report in regard to the evidence that was found at the scene of Stacy's murder. Hugh noticed his eyes darting left and right as he read every line. The man stared intensely at the evidence and who the hair belonged to. It was all starting to make sense to him now.

"Well? What does it say, sir?"

Cleveland remained quiet as if he was the only one in the room.

"Sir?" Hugh repeated.

"Hmm? Oh, sorry. Yeah," he simply replied.

Hugh Schpenus IV

"Who did it belong to?"

Cleveland sat down at his desk and tossed the letter and envelop aside. "This can't be," he declared as he clutched his chin. A look of concern and worry was smeared on his face like stale butter.

Suddenly his office phone rang. The vulgar ring was loud and abrupt, almost as if it was perfectly timed. Both Hugh and Cleveland stood in place while their eyes locked together. The ringing continued as they both stared at one another, then at the office phone as the light flashed rapidly signifying it was from an unknown number.

"Sir? Are you going to..." But before he could finish his sentence Cleveland held up his hand.

"Yeah, I am going to answer it," he snatched up the phone and brought it to his ear.

A heavy breath filled the other end. It was an eerie sound that left a cold chill against his neck. Cleveland stayed silent.

"Well, aren't you going to say hello?" the man asked.

"Who is this?"

Hugh Schpenus IV

"Oh, Cleveland," the man said. "You already know who I am. In fact, my name is written right there in that letter you have on your desk."

"How do you know what is on my desk huh? Can you see me?"

The man laughed, "You can say that. Just like you know who I am."

"I can't believe what I am reading. Is it really you?"

"Yes," the man replied.

"Schpenus?"

Chapter 14

The Schpenus Awakens

Hugh Schpenus IV

The ice-cold water splashed against my body. In the distance another explosion rocked against the blusterous sky. There was no storm cloud above me, just the remnants from an airplane crashing into the sea. My eyes barely opened wide enough to see the red parachute floating off, carried against the same wind that pushed me away from it. Cleveland was safe, but he thought I was far from it. That was fine. I'll let him think I'm dead. I could use the vacation.

Another explosion rocked me to sleep as I laid here on the broken metal debris from the plane. In the wreckage the woman simply known as Mama, was dead along with my past. Now that she's gone, along with my father and brother, I am the only Schpenus that remains. My father and brother were two men I hardly knew. I met my father briefly in Russia during my hunt for the criminal warlord who was actually my mother, Mama. Irony at its best. I closed my eyes and my body drifted away in what felt like an endless ocean.

"Are you alive?" the woman asked me.

I slowly opened my eyes to find two beautiful blue pearls staring down at me. Blonde hair danced in the breeze beneath her black baseball cap. Her pale skin told me wherever I was must be a

Hugh Schpenus IV

sun deprived place. Those eyes, blue and beautiful like two majestic shards of broken icicles. She smiled at me compassionately and repeated her question.

"Are you alive?"

She touched my numb and damp skin. I must've felt like a corpse and would have been mistaken for one if for not my sudden cough. Water escaped from my lungs and broken body. I opened my mouth to speak, but only more water spurted as if I were a human fountain on its last reservoir.

"Don't speak," she said and placed her hands on my body. She was warm to the touch.

"Where….am…I?" the only words I was able to speak.

"You are in Iceland. Reykjavik to be precise. This piece of debris carried you onto the shore. I was out fishing and noticed the reflection from this metal thing."

"Rey, what?" I asked, but slowly I faded out.

I awakened uncertain of what day it was or where I was. The wind howled against the small room. I was inside a wooden home. It was quaint and had that homey feel to it. The smell of a log burning in

Hugh Schpenus IV

the fireplace helped bring me back to reality. My naked body was covered beneath a heavy wool blanket. My muscles ached. My body felt like I ran ten marathons, but my memory reminded me of what really happened. I somehow survived the plane crash.

"You are awake," said my rescuer as she entered the room carrying a tray with a bowl of soup on it. She carefully set it down on the small table beside the bed. The aroma of rosemary and thyme tickled my senses.

"Where am I?" I asked her, sitting up exposing the top half of my body. My muscles were covered in bruises and scratches, remnants from the plane crash.

"You are in my home, in Reykjavik. Have you been to Iceland before?" she kindly asked me.

"No, I have not," I replied, then took a sip of my soup. The liquid warmed my body even more. "I thought this place would be covered in ice."

My remark invoked a laugh from her. "You are funny. Your accent, you are European?"

Hugh Schpenus IV

"Yes, I am from Austria originally, but I live in West End. It is a city in the United States."

"I am familiar with that place. I have a friend who owns an extermination store. Stop Bugging Me, I believe is the name."

Her words almost caused me to choke on my soup.

"Please, slow down, you are eating too fast," she said as she helped me back into bed. "You must rest."

"Your friend, he helped me with my mission."

"You are that guy? He wrote me a letter and told me about you ripping his uniforms," she said.

I smiled, "Yeah, I am that guy. But the world thinks I am dead now. And I intend to keep it that way."

"Why do you want to be dead?"

I looked at her and shook my head, "Because I need a vacation."

She laughed, "A vacation huh? What is your name?"

"Hugh Schpenus," I answered. "What is your name?"

"My name is Idunn Moorhead."

Hugh Schpenus IV

"That's an interesting name," I declared.

"I would say about yours. My father is from Scotland and moved here where he met my mother."

"I see, well, I suppose I should leave," I said while I attempted to get out of her bed. But before I could move any further a sharp pain erupted from my legs.

"No, please, you can stay. You are in no condition to leave."

"All right, I won't argue with you. I had a tough day anyway."

"I can see that," Idunn said while staring at my naked body.

"Oh! Sorry!" I declared while pulling the blanket over me.

"I think it's about time you tell me what happened. When I found you, you were almost dead Schpenus."

I smiled, "Okay, I will tell you what happened to me. Let me start from the beginning."

Hugh Schpenus IV

Chapter 15

Iceland Fifteen Years Later

It has been fifteen years since Idunn saved me and brought me back to life. The axe fell down like an angry hammer. Chopping away at the log, bit, by bit. My body was sweaty despite the air being near freezing. The wool sweater kept me warm and hot simultaneously. For the last fifteen years after the plane crash, I have been living in this country with Idunn Moorhead on her small farm.

Hugh Schpenus IV

Sheep bleated nearby as she directed them into a nearby shed for a haircut. She flashed her infectious smile as she stared at me happily.

I did not expect to not only survive that plane crash, but to find love. If Stacy could see me now, I wonder what he would say. He always wanted me to settle down with a beautiful woman who would treat me like a king. A part of me felt guilt and shame for trading the rugged hard life of dodging bullets for this simple life of chopping wood. The sound of an approaching car distracted me. I looked up and flipped my blonde hair back. My hair was now longer on one side. My beloved recommended I try to blend in like a local in hopes of no one figuring out my true identity.

As the red truck approached, I clutched the handle of the axe tightly. My instincts from the past kicked in. This is Reykjavik. The only crime that happens here is the unforgiving winters and early sunsets. I gently laid down the axe and approached the truck as it slowed down. The brakes lightly squeaked as it came to a stop.

"Here is your mail, Dick Raasch," said the postman.

"Thank you," I said, taking the mail from him.

"Have a great day, Dick Raasch," he declared.

Hugh Schpenus IV

"You too!" I replied as the truck drove off.

I smiled out of a mixture of annoyance and guilt at Idunn who exited from the shed.

"Ah, the mail arrived early today, huh? Dick," she smiled at me.

"I do not understand why I have this name. Do I look like a Dick Raasch to you?" I asked while giving her the mail.

My questions caused her to laugh. "No, but you are the one who said it is best to conceal your real name. Plus, it suits you," she added while slapping my behind with the mail.

"Yeah, I guess you are right. It sounds Austrian doesn't it?"

"You could say that. Come on let's go inside. It is going to snow, and I am hungry."

Inside, I sat on the couch and began flipping through the endless channels on the television. I could never get used to this. Satellite television. It amazed me that there is a thing flying above us.

"You can't get used to satellite television now? You better get used to things Mr. Raasch," Idunn said. She chuckled at me as she continued chopping vegetables.

Hugh Schpenus IV

"Do you need any help?" I asked.

"No, keep complaining and watching television, Dick."

I shook my head and continued flipping through the channels until I reached the news station from West End. "And in other news, the killer behind the murder of Stacy Jackson has been identified as Hugh Schpenus." The remote suddenly slipped out of my hand and crashed onto the wooden floor. I turned and looked at Idunn, who was already staring at me in shock. Her mouth was open, but she remained silent.

"How is this even possible?" she questioned while pointing the chopping knife at the television.

"I don't know, but Stacy is dead. And somehow, I am behind his murder. This doesn't make sense. I have been with you the whole time!"

"I know Dick, I mean Schpenus. I know," her words were filled with fear. She knew what I was going to do and there was no way she could stop me.

"You know what I have to do now, don't you?" I asked her.

Hugh Schpenus IV

She placed the knife on the counter and began weeping, "I don't want you to go alone. Please, take me with you. I can help you."

I stood up and held her against my chest. She wept even harder as the wool sweater saturated her tears like a sponge.

"I have to go, and I must do this alone," I declared. My words only angered her.

She pushed me away and turned her back while burying her face into her hands. I rested my hands on her shoulders and embraced her one last time.

"I will return to you my love, I promise."

"You better!" Idunn yelled, turning and returning the embrace. "If you don't, I will go to West End and find you myself!"

"I will find out who is behind this and make them pay!"

Chapter 16

Arrival

Hugh Schpenus IV

I arrived at the airport terminal in West End. I unbuttoned my black trench coat as I made my way to the exit. My passport, which had my alias, Dick Raasch, kept my true identity secret and safe. Whoever framed me must have known that I was alive. The first thing I wanted to do was to show up at the police station and talk to Cleveland. But my instincts told me that was a bad idea. If the news anchor was right, then that meant he must be out there looking for me. My only option was to lay low and find a place to stay. Plus, everyone still thought I was dead.

"Where to?" the cabdriver asked me as I entered the back seat.

"Take me to the Dolphin Motel over on Eighth Avenue."

"Oh, you know your places, huh? Sorry pal, but that place closed down fifteen years ago," the driver replied while eyeing me through the rearview mirror. "You haven't been here in a while, huh? How about the Rosebud? It's over on ninth near the police station."

"Sure, that sounds good."

As the car sped away from the airport, I stared out and looked at what has become of my city. There were even more skyscrapers

Hugh Schpenus IV

scattered throughout the downtown area now. I flicked my hair away from my face and sighed. This city seemed so foreign to me now. My eyes began to water at the thought of losing my friend. I needed to visit Stacy's grave to at least pay my respects to him.

"Where are you from pal? You look familiar. Have I seen you before?" asked the driver.

"No, I don't believe so. I have only been here once before, on business," I answered.

"Oh, where are you from?"

"Me? Well, I am from Iceland," I simply said.

"Oh yeah? I haven't been there, but man you must do a lot of ice skating."

I look over at him and noticed he was constantly eyeing me through the rearview mirror as if he were trying to figure out who I was.

"Why is that?"

"Huh? Oh, because isn't that country covered in ice?"

Hugh Schpenus IV

I laughed at his question, "No, that's Greenland. It's called Iceland to keep people from traveling there and go to Greenland instead so they can freeze. Greenland is not actually green at all."

"Huh? I don't get it," he declared. "What's your name pal? I'm Larry."

"Dick," I stated.

"Nice to meet you, Dick."

The rest of the ride the driver focused on taking me to my destination, which worked in my favor since I was not in the mood for simple chit-chatting. My mind began to wander, and I imagined what Cleveland must look like now. I also wondered about things at the police station and if he was still in charge. My curiosity was slowly gnawing and eating away at me. I needed to get in contact with him.

"Okay, here we are," the driver declared as we pulled up to the entrance of the Rosebud Motel.

"Thank you," I said.

After I paid the driver, I entered the small motel. The red carpet greeted me along with an antique chandelier that hung overhead with several paintings of rose gardens. The place looked like it was trying

Hugh Schpenus IV

too hard at attempting to be a classy hotel, but beneath this shell was a place for scumbags and lowlifes. It was the perfect cover for me.

"Hello, sir, welcome to the Rosebud. How many are in your party?" the woman asked me, taking my passport.

"Just me and I need three nights."

"Alright Mr. Raasch is it?" she asked me as she looked up and smiled provocatively.

"Yeah, but just call me Dick."

I checked into the hotel and made my way into the room, which smelled like cigarettes and bad memories. I wanted to leave, but this was the only place where I could unfortunately call my temporary home. With no one to contact, I decided my next plan before beginning my investigation was to visit Stacy's grave. But first, I had to call my beloved.

"Idunn?" I asked softly on my cellphone.

"Yes, you arrived! I was so worried!" she replied.

"Yeah, I am here. I am going to keep minimal contact with you just in case things get heavy here okay?"

Hugh Schpenus IV

"I don't know what that means, but you better call me again okay? Keep me updated."

"All right, I will."

"I love you dear, where are you going now?" Idunn asked, concerned and scared for me.

"I love you, too. I'm going to the cemetery to visit Stacy. I need to go. It will be dark soon and I want to get back by then."

"Please be home in three weeks, it will be Christmas you know."

"Yes, I will. Talk soon Idunn."

Hugh Schpenus IV

Chapter 17

Unexpected Encounter

With two hours left of sunlight, the cemetery was still open since it closed at sunset. With winter being upon us that meant it closed at four. This gave me just enough time to visit and pay my respects to my old friend. After I headed to the office and found out where he was buried, I walked toward his grave. I wanted to dress nicer but given the circumstances I had hoped my red and black flannel shirt and long black trench coat was appropriate.

Hugh Schpenus IV

The wind rushed around me as I stood there at my friend's grave. Stacy Jackson. He was the only one who believed in me long enough to see me grow into the best detective West End has ever known. Tears filled my eyes as my jacket danced in the cold wintry air. Vapor escaped my lungs as I exhaled deeply.

"My friend, I am sorry I wasn't there to say goodbye. Someone is out to get me. I have spent the last fifteen years in retirement," I said. A chuckle escaped me at the word. "Retirement. It never really fit you know, boss? I miss you sir, and I am sorry I wasn't here to save you. Whoever took your life must pay. I will find out who is behind this, and why they are using me as a scapegoat. But you and I both know that I had nothing to do with your murder."

Suddenly footsteps approached from behind. I turned around and locked eyes with an unexpected visitor. It was my friend, Michael Cleveland. Upon seeing my presence, his eyes widened with both shock and anger. Without saying anything to me he unholstered his gun and aimed directly at me. A sight I never thought I would ever see or experience. My own friend holding and aiming his peacemaker at me.

"You! You are under arrest!" he angrily yelled.

Hugh Schpenus IV

"Cleveland, listen to me, it wasn't me! I just got here!"

"Stop it Schpenus, you called me yesterday and told me everything. I have seen the DNA; the evidence is all solid. We both know you are behind this!"

"What DNA? What phone call? I don't understand!"

"Look, we can do this the easy way or the hard way. I don't want to shoot you, but I will if I have to! So don't make me do it!"

I held up my black gloved hands, "I don't know what you are talking about, but I spent the last fifteen years in Iceland. I can show you my passport," I said, slowly opening my jacket.

"Don't you move!" Cleveland declared, cocking the handgun. "Don't make any sudden movements!"

"All right, but listen, I am not armed."

He scoffed at my statement, "Then you are a damn fool for coming here. Why are you here huh? You killed this man. What business do you have coming here?" he slowly stepped toward me.

"I arrived here today, and I wanted to pay my respects."

Hugh Schpenus IV

"You wanted to pay your respects? You killed this man! You are not making sense!"

"Exactly! Because I didn't do it!"

"Whatever Hugh, you were a brother to me! I loved you like a brother, just like he did!" he glanced over at Stacy's grave. "And on top of that you killed Tina! Are you going to go pay your respects to her, too?"

"Tina is dead? What?"

"Oh, come on man! Don't play dumb with me! Cut this act out!"

I sighed. Up until now I had no idea Tina was dead. Granted we had a year of romance, but still, it stung me to know my friend was dead.

"You know, your son doesn't know." Cleveland approached closer.

I shook my head at his words, "Son? What son? I do not understand. I have a son?"

"Yes you do! Hugh Jass, but I won't tell him. No, I will leave that task to you. You need to tell him why you killed his mother."

"Tina is his mother?" I asked.

Hugh Schpenus IV

Knowing if I ran it would only make me look further guilty considering the circumstances. Plus, I needed to find out who this Hugh Jass was. Seeing my friend alive and well, it made me happy despite the situation. I gave Cleveland a cold and long stare.

"I don't know what you are talking about Cleveland, but I will go with you," I declared while I held out my hands. "But I ask of one thing."

"You're in no condition to make demands, but I will hear you out," he said, placing the handcuffs around my wrists.

"Run my passport, and you will see that I am not lying to you."

Chapter 18

Unexpected News

He stood in the small room and continued lifting the heavy dumbbells. Sweat poured down his body as the television blared behind him. His short and spikey blonde hair reflected the setting sun. A smile stretched across his face as the news anchor declared the news.

Hugh Schpenus IV

"And in late breaking news, the one and only Hugh Schpenus has been caught. It is a shame how this once beloved cop has fallen from grace. Why he committed these two heinous murders remain a mystery, but hopefully we can find out in the coming days." The camera panned and briefly showed Cleveland standing outside the police station. "Listen, I don't have anything further to add, but we got the bastard. He's not going to be treated differently than the other scumbags. When I have something, I will share it with you all."

The man dropped the dumbbells onto the floor and stretched his arms out. He stared contently at the television screen and laughed. His plan was working perfectly especially since the sudden and surprise appearance of Hugh Schpenus was an added bonus. The assassin did not expect to see the man alive, but for him to take the fall and blame was perfect. At least this meant the heat was now off of him.

"Did you see the news?" he asked, holding his cellphone. "Yes, I know. I thought he was dead, too. Shall we take both of them then?"

"Yes, of course, they both must die!" the younger man answered on the other end of the phone.

Hugh Schpenus IV

"I can take care of them both. I have the hardware and the leftover army from my mother."

"You Russians and your mercenary armies. Fine, take your men and take them both out. If you fail…."

The assassin interrupted, "I will not fail. I have a Gatling gun with hundreds of bullets."

"You will need every single bullet to take out a Schpenus."

Hugh Schpenus IV

Chapter 19

Impossible

"Run it again!" Cleveland yelled. "This isn't possible! How the hell was he in Iceland when he called me two days ago?"

"I don't know sir, but it checks out!" Katerini answered.

"Checks out my ass. This doesn't make any sense! Have you seen Hugh Jass?"

"I have, he went to talk to the suspect."

"He what? Oh damn, I gotta go down there. Keep the press at bay, I am going to go down to the cells," ordered Cleveland.

Hugh Schpenus IV

Meanwhile, I sat in my cell. The police let me keep my attire since I was being held there temporarily until they set my court date. This worked out for me since the cell was cold, so my jacket and jeans kept me warm enough. Since this was such a high-profile case, I was the only one in the jail cells. They put me at the furthest one, which meant I was in cell four.

"So, you're Hugh Schpenus, huh?" said the young man who stood in front of my cell. He wore a black leather jacket, white tank top, blue jeans, and black boots. He eyed me as if he was sizing me up for a fight.

"Yeah, who are you?" I asked nicely.

"I am Hugh Jass. You killed my mother."

"I did not kill anyone. Look, I am sorry for your loss. Tina was my friend, too."

"Don't you dare," he replied. "You were never her friend! You took her from me!"

"Look kid, I didn't kill anyone. I have been framed!"

"Whatever! I am going to kill you right now," he declared, then reached for his sidearm.

Hugh Schpenus IV

"Hey Hugh Jass," Cleveland called out. "Get the hell out of here son. Go and take a breather."

The young detective looked over and then looked at me again. He shook his head, sighed, and walked away.

I felt bad for him. He was angry at the wrong person. Seeing Tina's son also made me wonder if it were true. Was I really his father? He looked somewhat like me, but it did not add up. I was not romantically involved with Tina. Plus, when I met her, he would have been born already.

"So, that's him huh?" I asked.

"Yeah, poor kid huh?" Cleveland answered while rubbing his stubby chin.

"You know, you look good bald," I said. "I mean, don't get me wrong, I do miss the afro, too."

My words brought an unexpected chuckle. "You know, despite the circumstances, it is good to see you alive."

"Oh? So, you're not mad at me anymore?" I politely asked.

"I like the hair," he declared. "It's a lot longer than before."

Hugh Schpenus IV

"Thanks. The spikey hair thing outgrew me."

"Here's your passport, Dick Raasch," he said and tossed my passport at me. "Nice name."

I laughed, "Thanks, my wife gave it to me."

"Wife huh? When the hell did that happen?"

"Fifteen years ago, after she rescued me."

Cleveland shook his head, "I cannot believe this man, not only are you alive, but someone framed you. I also cannot believe that I am about to say this, but you are free to go. Despite the evidence we have against you, you are innocent. There is no way in hell you killed anyone since you weren't even here."

"What evidence did you have against me?" I asked as my friend opened my cell. The metal door squeaked lightly as I exited.

"The kid found some DNA at the scene, a lock of hair."

"Hair huh? Strange, how did he find my hair when I wasn't even here."

"That's what I would like to know. Come on let's go talk to him."

Hugh Schpenus IV

Chapter 20

Peppermint

As we headed upstairs a loud explosion shook the police station. Cleveland and I exchanged looks before we ran up the stairs. Another stronger explosion rang out shaking the walls and ceiling sending fragments of debris on us. Gunfire rang out shortly after we entered the main floor. The explosion knocked out the electricity in the building, which made it difficult for us to find our way through the station. Bullets whizzed by and ricocheted as the two of us navigating toward his office.

Hugh Schpenus IV

"I have some weapons stored away including one of your favorites," declared Cleveland. "Follow me and stay low."

In the distance the sound of automatic gunfire continued to ring out, followed by handgun fire, which I assumed was the police officers.

"In here," ordered Cleveland. "Shut the door behind you."

The two of us entered his office, and while crouched, I closed his office door and locked it. Suddenly flood lights turned on throughout the station revealing everything inside the office. Cleveland hurried over to a large wooden cabinet and opened it, revealing a large cache of weapons. Outside gunfire continued forcing me to take cover behind his former boss' desk.

"Hey, what's this?" I asked, noticing the picture of him and his father.

"That? That was in the letter you mailed to me shortly after the plane crash," answered Cleveland who was rummaging through the cabinet.

"What? I never mailed you any letter." I picked up the frame and studied the photo. "I remember this day. It was shortly before the accident."

"Accident? What accident?"

Hugh Schpenus IV

"There was a car accident and my brother died. Anyway, I did not send you this."

"Well damn, I don't know who did then. Here take this," said Cleveland. He tossed over a familiar weapon to his friend.

The sight of the shotgun brought a smile to my face as if I were a child unwrapping a Nintendo on Christmas morning. "Where in the hell did you get this? I love her!"

Cleveland smiled, "I knew you would be happy to be reunited with your gun. What was her name again?"

"Peppermint," I answered while flashing a huge smile and still staring at the shotgun.

"Peppermint huh? Why?" he asked me.

I stood up clutching the shotgun against my chest. It felt like I was reunited with a lost love.

"Because she peppers some nice spice. Just watch," I proclaimed. I cocked the shotgun and kicked the office door open.

"Hey, you owe me a new door!" Cleveland declared.

I turned and looked at my friend, "Bill me."

Hugh Schpenus IV

Outside the office, several officers were huddled behind desks while others were down on the floor. Schpenus spotted several men dressed in black tactical gear and black ski masks. All of them were wielding the classic mercenary weapons, submachine guns, AK-47s, and even P90 machine guns.

"Look! There he is!" one of the mercenaries yelled, pointing his assault rifle in my direction.

"Here I am!" I barked back, firing several shots from the shotgun.

The bullets sprayed out in every direction hitting two of the men, causing a barrage of cackling return gunfire. I was forced to take cover behind a nearby desk. Bullets ricocheted and dinged off the desk and walls.

"You need a hand?" Cleveland asked, stepping out of his office. In his hands he held two machine guns. "I have two right here," he said while the guns erupted in a barrage of gunfire.

More of the mercenaries went down with ease as the bullets littered the area. Shell casings dinged and fell onto the floor by Cleveland's shoes. After he emptied the ammo clips, the man joined me and reloaded his guns.

Hugh Schpenus IV

"Nice guns, what are their names?" I asked, still reloading my Peppermint.

"This right here," he answered, holding up one of the black machine guns, "Is named Ass. And this other one," he said, holding up the other machine gun, "Is named Kicker."

Chapter 21

The Unmasked Assassin

The remaining mercenaries continued focusing their guns on us, forcing us to stay pinned down behind the abandoned police desk.

"We need to get out of here," suggested Cleveland. "Wait a minute, Kate, is that you?"

Hugh Schpenus IV

Katerini laid toward the front of the main area of the station beside one of the turned over desks. She leaned against the desk, clutching her shoulder tightly and wincing in pain.

"Yeah, I'll be fine. Just a flesh wound, boss."

"Hold on, we'll be right there." He looked at me and said, "Cover me."

As the man crouched and began scurrying through the labyrinth of desks, two mercenaries noticed his movement and began firing their AK-47s at him. Bullets whizzed by Cleveland, but he continued forward. If he slowed down to return fire, he would chance being shot from one of the bullets.

"I got you, boss," I yelled, firing multiple shots from my shotgun. The loud booms drowned out the sound of their assault rifles. I continued firing at them until their guns could no longer be heard. "I'm out, I gotta reload my Peppermint!"

Luckily, Cleveland reached Katerini, who had been shot in the shoulder. She smiled the moment he joined her at the makeshift hiding spot she made. Dried blood rested against her beautiful face.

"Are you all right? Let me see it," he asked, gently inspecting her gunshot wound. "Oh, yeah, you will be fine."

Hugh Schpenus IV

"I told you, boss, it's just a flesh wound."

Deep down, Cleveland noticed her attempt at hiding the pain. She was a tough cop and he was proud to have her on his team. She worked hard and was a strong-willed woman who took no pity from anyone. She was determined to not only make him proud but herself, too.

"Here, take one of these and call me in the morning," he declared, handing her one of his machine guns.

"Gee, thanks boss, I feel better already," she answered sarcastically.

"This is the best I can do under these circumstances. How many cops do we have left?"

"Not many, boss, most of them were taken out in the first wave. It looks like you two handled most of the remaining mercs."

"Where the hell is Hugh? Have you seen him?"

"No, sir, I haven't. I don't know where he is."

"Damn, now is when we need him most. Let me try him on the radio." he grabbed her radio but noticed the bullet hole in the middle.

"Oh yeah about that, it's kind of broken."

Hugh Schpenus IV

Cleveland shook his head, "I can see that. Damn. Okay, stay put. I will be back."

As he stood up, the remaining five mercenaries all began firing in unison at Cleveland forcing him to take cover across from Kate. I provided cover fire, directly hitting two of the men. The loud boom of the shotgun could be felt within my chest. The powerful gun was living up to its name since the men were succumbing to its will. Cleveland stood up and in unison with Kate, the two of them fired the machine guns at the remaining men.

One by one the men fell to the ground. It was almost like shooting fish in a barrel. The rattling gunfire from both the machine guns and assault rifles slowly ceased. All of the mercenaries that attacked the police station were defeated, or so they thought.

"Is that all of them?" Cleveland asked. "Good, I am out of ammo anyway," he declared.

"I think so, strange. Is it me or was this too easy?" I asked, placing my shotgun on the floor beside my black boots.

"Yeah something ain't right," he answered me.

Hugh Schpenus IV

"Knock, knock," announced the man, entering the front entrance of the police station. He surveyed the large room and could see several bodies consisting of both fallen police officers and his own mercenaries. "Wow, looks like I am late to the party." In his hands, he clutched a large Gatling gun. The bullets clung symphonically as they hung lifelessly from the end of the massive gun.

The mysterious figure stood beneath the blinding floodlights preventing us from seeing his face and identifying who he was. All we could see was his attire, which was a black leather jacket, a white tank top, blue jeans, and black boots. His face was difficult to make out, but his voice sounded familiar.

"Hugh, is it me, or does this guy sound really familiar?" Cleveland asked me.

"He does. Hey, who the hell are you?" I questioned.

"Oh? Do you want to find out? First, let me formally introduce myself," he answered.

Suddenly, the barrel began spinning wildly causing a loud whirring noise. The man laughed hysterically, waving the barrel of the gun left and right at both Cleveland and me.

Hugh Schpenus IV

"Get down!" I yelled.

The Gatling gun exploded in a barrage of gunfire sending hundreds of bullets at us both as we ducked behind a wall of several tipped over desks. The bullets relentlessly gnawed away at everything they touched. Pieces of concrete broke apart as the bullets danced against the walls and pillars inside the police station. Picture frames and office equipment were tossed into the air by the furious bullets. The force also damaged the computer monitors and pushed them off the desks and onto the floor.

The three of us continued cowering behind the continued onslaught from the menacing weapon. It felt like a never-ending barrage of bullets as they dinged onto the floor beside the man, who was smiling maniacally at the sight of the damage he was causing. With the last of the bullets running through the gun, the mysterious villain slowly came out from beneath the floodlights and away from the front entrance. He cautiously stepped over and around the bodies of the fallen with the last of the rounds draining from the loud whirring barrel.

As the gun came to a sputtering end, the barrel smoked like a veteran chain smoker inside a dive bar. Disappointed his joyride came to an end, the man tossed the heavy weapon aside onto the floor. A

Hugh Schpenus IV

loud thud echoed in the eerie silence left behind from the seven minutes of continuous gunfire. Pieces of concrete that dangled against the exposed iron rods fell and crumbled.

"So, are you still alive?" he asked, a hint of excitement hung in his voice.

"I am," I answered as I stood up from my hiding spot.

Cleveland joined me as we came face to face with their villain.

"What? How? It can't be! You're dead!" I declared while staring at the man.

"I guess it runs in the family," he replied, smiling happily at me. "I thought you were dead"

Hugh Schpenus IV

Chapter 22

Face to Face

"Wait a minute, are you telling me this guy is your twin brother?" Cleveland asked, shocked from the sight before his eyes. The man looked like a mirror image of Hugh Schpenus, except his blonde hair was short and spikey like the way his used to be back in his youthful days.

"I am," he answered. "Hello dear brother."

"I don't understand. Why are you doing this?" I asked.

Hugh Schpenus IV

"This wasn't about you brother; it was about revenge. But now that you are here, the revenge will just be that much sweeter."

Cleveland stood petrified in shock, "He even sounds like you Hugh, Austrian accent and all."

The man laughed, "No, I am Russian. Hugh is the Austrian one. Tell him, brother, tell him who I am."

"His name is Harry Schpenus," I declared. "But you were supposedly killed in the explosion."

"That explosion was no accident. Our father did that. He was trying to kill Mama, but luckily, she knew about his plan. Instead, she used me as a decoy. My supposed death pushed him away. But, without warning, it also pushed you away from us. Now, look at you, policeman Schpenus."

"But where were you when…" I paused.

"When you killed Mama? I was away on a mission. When I returned, I learned you kidnapped and killed her. But don't worry, I am here to avenge her."

"I don't understand, it was you that I saw! At the cemetery? The parking garage?" Cleveland asked.

Hugh Schpenus IV

Harry laughed, "Yes, I was haunting you like a ghost. That moment at the cemetery, I was hiding behind the tree ready to end your life. It was disappointing to see you turn around. But this moment was worth the wait. Plus, it worked perfectly since it brought my brother back from the dead. Did you receive my letter? That was also me."

"The photograph with the initials? That was you? Wait a minute, this means you killed Stacy and Tina! You're a monster!" Cleveland yelled. "I will kill you myself!"

Harry laughed at the man, who charged forward at him like an enraged bull. But Cleveland underestimated his opponent because before he could attack, Harry Schpenus gave him a quick hook kick to the face. The move combined with Cleveland's momentum flipped up around and onto the floor.

"Your turn, brother!" Harry excitedly stated.

I shook my head, "You are not my twin brother! You died a long time ago!"

I charged at my twin cautiously because I knew my brother was trained in various fighting styles as I was, which meant we were equally matched. Deciding it was best to take a soft offensive measure, I started out with a front kick, roundhouse kick combination

Hugh Schpenus IV

with my lead leg. Harry deflected both kicks with ease, then returned a powerful sidekick, but I gracefully skipped back dodging the attack. Harry smiled at my gracefulness.

"Looks like you still remember your training. This should be fun, brother."

"You are a psychopath Harry, just like Mama!"

My words rubbed him the wrong way like a drunk one-night stand. Harry came charging at me with a jumping front kick, then carried the momentum further with a left hook. I experienced difficulty blocking both attacks, but luckily, I barely managed. We both stepped back momentarily in concert to remove our black jackets.

"It's getting hot in here," declared Harry, tossing his black leather jacket onto the floor. "I never liked leather jackets. They feel quite vintage."

I ignored my brother's arrogant remark and tossed my black wool trench coat onto the floor revealing my black and a red checkered button-down shirt.

We both appeared in similar attire except our shirts were different. We could have passed for twins, but my long hair made it

Hugh Schpenus IV

easy to separate and distinguish the two of us. When we spoke there was also a stark difference in our accents since I was raised in Austria while Harry was raised in Russia.

"Okay, let's see who hits who first. We used to play this game as children remember?" Harry asked me.

I ignored my brother's arrogance and decided it was time for me to attack with greater force. With one swift motion, I attacked with a jump kick, but my brother was ready yet again. As the jump kick came flying in, Harry raised his arm and blocked his brother's attack gracefully. He then followed up with a roundhouse kick, striking me directly in the back. With the combined momentum of both my attack and Harry's counterattack, I found myself flying awkwardly onto a desk. The weight and force from my body caused the desk to collapse like a house of cards.

Harry laughed, "You are no match for me my brother. Give up, I have won. This fight is pointless since we are family!"

"Family huh?" Cleveland asked, approached Harry with a barrage of fists.

His unexpected attack caught Harry off guard. The first two fists met their mark, his face. But Harry quickly regained his balance

Hugh Schpenus IV

and managed to guard and deflect the other two attacks. Cleveland, surprised by the man's quick reflexes, knew he was no match for Hugh's brother. Despite him being a tad smaller in size, the man made up for it in speed.

"So, you want to dance, too? Okay, let's dance cowboy!"

Chapter 23

Final Fight

Harry kicked Cleveland in the stomach with his front leg. The force of the attack nearly made the man vomit, but he held strong and allowed his adrenaline to take hold. He staggered back, but Harry did not let up, and continued a swarm of kicks. He threw a strong hook kick aimed at Cleveland's head, which connected with ease. Surprised by the man's strength and ability to kick high, Cleveland felt lightheaded but still did his best to hold his own. He clumsily attacked with a left hook, but Harry caught his arm and swung himself around the man.

With his arms coiled around Cleveland's neck, he administered a sleeper hold on him. Cleveland knew he could not succumb to this because this meant it was lights out for good. With a strong thrust, he drove his elbow at Harry's stomach while wrapping his leg around the man's ankle. As Cleveland continued driving his elbow into Harry's body, he used his bodyweight and pushed back forcing him into a

Hugh Schpenus IV

concrete pillar. With his back pressed against the pillar, Harry held on like a ravenous Pitbull.

Cleveland smiled. "How do you like this?" he asked, gasping for consciousness, and lifted his head back into Harry's face. The force of the attack pushed his head into the pillar causing him to loosen his grip on Cleveland's neck. Seeing a way out, he released a quick back kick into Harry's groin causing a wince from the man.

Unable to speak, Harry clutched his groin and began gasping from the pain he was enduring. Cleveland wanted to continue attacking, but he was too busy regaining his breath. The two men eyed each other like lions fighting over a fresh kill. Harry smiled maniacally revealing a mouthful of blood and saliva. The attack broke his nose and several teeth, but this also left a lingering sharp pain at the back of Cleveland's bald head. He missed the cushion his hair used to provide.

"Not bad, Cleveland, not bad at all. Are you ready for round two?"

He shook his head at Harry, "You really don't know when to give up do you?"

Hugh Schpenus IV

"Schpenuses never quit!" he proclaimed. The question somehow sparked another surge of hate inside of him. Harry charged forward like a football player.

The speed he exhibited was too quick for Cleveland to counter. Instead he braced himself for the tackle. Harry drove his shoulder into him like a tackling linebacker. With inhuman like strength, Harry lifted the man off the floor and drove him forward into a cubicle. The force from the tackle and the weight from their bodies combined, caused the cubicle to collapse like a child's dollhouse.

Cleveland felt something sharp penetrate his side, but he was too tired to figure out what it was. He slowly opened his eyes and through the floodlights, Harry stood over him smiling and laughing evilly. His shadow casted over him like a winter solar eclipse, but instead of losing his vision, Cleveland was losing blood.

"Looks like I beat you, Cleveland. Are you ready to die?" he asked with clenched fists.

"Not if I have something to say about that!" I yelled.

I wrapped my pythonic arms around my brother's stomach and like a wrestler, I lifted the man up into the air. Using my full momentum and strength, I suplexed Harry into another desk containing several

Hugh Schpenus IV

computer equipment including monitors and towers. The surprise attack caught Harry off guard leaving him lying on broken debris of wood and glass from the monitor. The crash was so loud, Cleveland looked up and wondered what had just happened. He wondered which brother was being suplexed.

The move left me damaged because part of my upper body fell into a computer chair, which collapsed on impact like a toy. I felt a great deal of stinging pain running through my upper back. As he stood up, Harry came charging forward diving into my body. But this time, I was ready for my brother's attack. As he pushed me back into another cubicle, I began driving my sharp elbows into his back. The attacks slowed him down momentarily until Harry managed to lift me off the floor and into another cubicle.

But luckily, the cubicle remained intact since it fell flat onto the floor beside shards of glass from a nearby broken window. As the glass crunched, I noticed a shard beside my hand. Before I reached for it, Harry wrapped his hands around my neck like an anaconda. As he began squeezing my neck, I stared directly into the man's blue eyes.

"It's time to end this fight and your life brother!" Harry declared, laughing maniacally. "This is for Mama! I will see you in hell!"

Hugh Schpenus IV

Feeling myself beginning to lose consciousness, I smiled at my twin brother. My unexpected smile left him surprised and confused.

"Why are you smiling at me? Are you embracing death?"

"No," I answered weakly. I clutched the glass shard and said, "I always thought you were a glasshole!"

Without hesitation, I drove the shard of glass into Harry's chest. The attack forced him to refocus his hands onto the shard protruding from his body. He tried pulling it out, but I followed up with a side kick aimed directly at the end of the glass. The attack sent him flying into the break room door. This time I was going to make sure my brother died.

"Stick around," I said to my brother, who was hanging lifelessly from the wooden door. I turned around and helped my best friend up, "Are you all right?"

Cleveland smiled, "Yeah, I will be fine, go and help Kate."

I nodded and went to help Kate.

"Hey Hugh, let's get the hell out of here. I don't want to die in here."

Hugh Schpenus IV

With Kate's arms around my shoulder, I smiled at Cleveland and replied, "Yeah let's get out of here."

Chapter 24

Outside

The late-night air greeted us as we staggered outside the front of the police station and into the parking lot. Cleveland clutched his side, which was bleeding profusely. I walked in pain while clutching Kate's body. She was barely alive but hanging on strong.

"Hey Hugh, we really shook the pillars tonight, huh?" Cleveland asked weakly.

"Yeah, come on, my car is right over…" I paused and in concert, we looked up at the approaching helicopter.

The helicopter slowly lowered itself in the distance.

"Oh, that must be Hugh Jass, he is here to help us!" Kate happily announced.

"Yeah! Jass! We're over here!" Cleveland yelled while waving his arms.

Hugh Jass sat in the helicopter and flipped several switches up. The helicopter paused and hovered briefly like a hummingbird in front of a flower. But instead of coming to our rescue, something else happened instead, a rocket was released. It streaked out like a snake leaving behind a line of smoke. After the first one was released, a second followed closely behind.

Hugh Schpenus IV

"What the hell is he doing?" Cleveland asked as the three of us stared in disbelief at the approaching rockets.

"Get down!" I yelled.

As the three of us dove forward onto the cold asphalt the two rockets flew directly over and into the police station. A large explosion broke out sending flames and debris in every direction. Shards of glass and debris rained down like an unnatural storm. The force of the explosion was loud and dazzled the night sky.

Still, in shock from what transpired, I crawled with Kate toward a parked police car. Cleveland, who was covered by large pieces of debris from the police station, laid still. Worried for him, I had to help my friend.

I looked at Kate, "Are you okay?"

"Yeah, I am. Go, check on Cleveland."

"Okay, I will be right back!" I said, cautiously running toward Cleveland.

With his body out in the open, Hugh Jass aimed and began firing a heavy machine gun at me. The bullets dinged and ricocheted off the asphalt narrowly missing me. I knew if I continued toward

Hugh Schpenus IV

Cleveland, I risked him getting shot so instead, I turned and ran for cover by another police car. The bullets followed close behind as I ran at full speed despite the pain throbbing within my back.

Now leaning against the driver's side of a parked police car, I braced myself as the bullets bounced off the roof and passenger side. As the windows shattered raining pieces of window onto my body, all I could do was stare ahead at my friend, who was slowly beginning to move.

"Hugh," Cleveland called out weakly.

"Yeah, I am here, don't move. Hugh Jass is shooting at us."

"I know, he thinks you killed his mother. But Hugh, you are his father."

He shook his head, "No, I am not Cleveland. His father is Harry Schpenus."

"Are you sure?" Cleveland asked, slowly crawling out from the fallen debris on his body.

"Yeah, I am sure trust me. I would know if he was one of mine."

My remark brought a chuckle out of Cleveland. "Then I won't feel so bad about giving you this," he added.

Hugh Schpenus IV

"What are you giving me?" I asked.

"Take this," he answered, sliding a small revolver handgun over to him.

I picked up the handgun and shook my head, "Cleveland, what do you expect me to do with this? I can't take out that helicopter with this peashooter."

Cleveland groaned, "Hugh, look at where the helicopter his hovering near."

Confused by my friend's words, I cautiously turned and glanced through the broken windows of the police car. It was at that moment when I spotted exactly what Cleveland was seeing. The helicopter was hovering near an electrical pole with power lines dangling near its top rotor. I knew I had to move in and get close enough to shoot the power lines. I returned to cover just as the bullets rang out again and struck the police car. As more shards of glass from the windows came down, dinging off the asphalt, I looked over at his friend, who was barely conscious. Time was running out.

It was at that moment when something unexpected happened, a feeling began to form inside of me like an abrupt storm. I glanced over and saw my nephew staring back at me, rage-filled his eyes. But

Hugh Schpenus IV

it was a misplaced and misguided rage. Like a poisonous seed planted in his heart. Despite having the clear advantage of the opportunity to brutally end this, I surveyed the area. There was Cleveland, lying on the asphalt barely alive. The police station, which was a second home to me, burned in the distance like fading memories. Enough bloodshed and innocent lives were lost that day. Enough destruction was done. I did not want to have my nephew dead on my hands. Taking a chance, I stood up and held my arms up while staring directly at my nephew. The helicopter hovered as he aimed the large automatic weapon at me.

"I am here! If you want to kill me then at least let me tell you something before you do it!" I yelled.

Intrigued by my words, Hugh Jass disappeared from view. Carefully, he lowered the helicopter onto the street and part of the parking lot. Behind me, I could still feel the heat from the raging fire. Slowly the large whirling rotor came to a stop as my nephew stepped out from the helicopter. He wore a black blazer with matching slacks and a shirt. His features were striking between my brother and his mother, Tina.

"You want to chit chat? Well let's chit chat," he said, flashing a Glock in his hand.

Hugh Schpenus IV

Chapter 25

Revelations

"Tell me why I shouldn't shoot you right here, right now, where you stand?" Jass aimed the gun at me as his anger took hold of him like a ravenous snake.

I dropped my handgun onto the parking lot, still keeping my eyes focused on my nephew, "I am not going to shoot you."

Hesitation lingered. He contemplated. "What's your angle? Why are you giving up so easily?"

Hugh Schpenus IV

I smiled at my nephew, "I never said I was. There is something you must know. I know who your father is."

My words caused him to step closer while still holding his aim toward me.

"Yeah? Let me guess, you are my father? The next thing you will tell me is that I can move objects with my hand."

I laughed, "No, I am serious."

"Okay, and? Who is my father? You?"

"No, I am your uncle."

Hugh Jass laughed at my response, "You? My uncle? Please, tell me another lie."

"Your father is a Schpenus. But it is not me. His name is Harry Schpenus."

A look of confusion was painted across his face. "What? But the evidence I found."

"Yes, the evidence you found pinpointed a Schpenus at the scene of the crime. It could have been either of us since we are twins."

Hugh Schpenus IV

He shook his head, "No, you are lying!" the sound of denial rested heavy in my nephew's voice.

"I understand this is difficult to accept, but I am not lying to you." I held out my hand, "Please, put the weapon down, and come with me."

Hugh Jass scoffed, "And what, spend the rest of my days locked in a cage like some animal? No, I would rather…" he hesitated to finish his words.

"Listen, you will not be alone. I will be here be with you every step of the way. Trust me." I smiled at my nephew as he slowly lowered the gun. "We are family."

In the distance the flashing red and blue strobe lights filled the last specks of night in the air from the emergency, which looked like a techno party. As the gun slipped out of his fingers, I cautiously approached him and took the weapon away from him. It was finally over.

Hugh Schpenus IV

Chapter 26

Reunited

The sun hung high over the bay in West End today. It was a beautiful and perfect day. The air was the perfect temperature, too, not too cold or hot, but just right. Outside we gathered together celebrating the Cleveland's return. He walked with a subtle limp, but we ignored it and smiled because today was the day of days. Sailboats slowly passed by along the sparkling crystal-like ocean waters. Gulls cried out as they flew above us.

"Well, well, look at all of these smiling faces!" Cleveland proclaimed as he lifted his beer. He wore a canary yellow colored short sleeve shirt, brown slacks, and a black Newsboy cap. One thing about my friend,

Hugh Schpenus IV

he always knew how to show up in full style. It warmed my heart seeing him here with us smiling brightly.

"He looks good, huh?" Katerini asked me as she held a glass of red wine. She looked amazing in her light purple summer dress, which was adorned with colorful flowers.

"He sure does! Hey, and what's this I hear about you two?" I asked her.

My question caused her to slightly blush.

"Yeah," she answered quietly. "It sort of just happened while he was in the hospital. Don't tell him, but I am expecting twins."

I laughed and shook my head, "You better break this news to him gently because he may faint! I almost did!"

"Okay, everyone come on!" Cleveland said. "Everyone gather around, I want to make a toast."

We all stood in front of him and raised our glasses.

"To the fallen, let them not be forgotten, but always remembered," he declared.

Hugh Schpenus IV

Hugh Schpenus IV